Flower Fairies of the Spring

POEMS AND PICTURES BY

CICELY MARY BARKER

D1187069

BLACKIE: LONDON AND GLASGOW

SPRING MAGIC

The World is very old;
　　But year by year
It groweth new again
　　When buds appear.

The World is very old,
　　And sometimes sad;
But when the daisies come
　　The World is glad.

The World is very old;
　　But every Spring
It groweth young again,
　　And fairies sing.

Distributed in the United States by
Two Continents Publishing Group Ltd.,
30 East 42nd Street, New York, NY 10017

copyright
All rights reserved

Blackie & Son Ltd., Bishopbriggs, Glasgow
450 Edgware Road, London W2 1EG

Printed in Great Britain by Smith and Ritchie Ltd., Edinburgh.

CONTENTS

The Snowdrop Fairy   4
The Hazel-Catkin Fairy   6
The Coltsfoot Fairy   8
The Dead-Nettle Fairy   10
The Celandine Fairy   12
The Willow-Catkin Fairy   14
The Groundsel Fairy   16
The Windflower Fairy   18
The Shepherd's-Purse Fairy   20
The Daisy Fairy   22
The Dandelion Fairy   24
The Daffodil Fairy   26
The Dog-Violet Fairy   28
The Primrose Fairy   30
The Lady's Smock Fairy   32
The Larch Fairy   34
The Bluebell Fairy   36
The Stitchwort Fairy   38
The Wood-Sorrel Fairy   40
The Speedwell Fairy   42
The Lords-and-Ladies Fairy   44
The Cowslip Fairy   46
The Hearts-Ease Fairy   48
The May Fairy   50

THE SONG OF
THE SNOWDROP FAIRY

Deep sleeps the Winter, cold, wet, and grey;
Surely all the world is dead; Spring is far
away.
Wait! the world shall waken; it is not dead,
for lo,
The Fair Maids of February stand in the
snow!

The Snowdrop Fairy

THE SONG OF
THE HAZEL-CATKIN FAIRY

Like little tails of little lambs,
　　On leafless twigs my catkins swing;
They dingle-dangle merrily
　　Before the wakening of Spring.

Beside the pollen-laden tails
　　My tiny crimson tufts you see,
The promise of the autumn nuts
　　Upon the slender hazel tree.

While yet the woods lie grey and still
　　I give my tidings: " Spring is near!"
One day the land shall leap to life
　　With fairies calling: " Spring is *here*!"

The Hazel-Catkin Fairy

THE SONG OF
THE COLTSFOOT FAIRY

The winds of March are keen and cold;
I fear them not, for I am bold.

I wait not for my leaves to grow;
They follow after: they are slow.

My yellow blooms are brave and bright;
I greet the Spring with all my might.

The Coltsfoot Fairy

THE SONG OF
THE DEAD-NETTLE FAIRY

Through sun and rain, and country lane,
The field, the road, are my abode.
Though leaf and bud be splashed with mud,
Who cares? Not I!—I see the sky,
The kindly sun, the wayside fun
Of tramping folk who smoke and joke,
The bairns who heed my dusty weed
(No sting have I to make them cry),
And truth to tell, they love me well.
My brothers, White, and Yellow bright,
Are finer chaps than I, perhaps;
Who cares? Not I! So now good-bye.

The Dead-Nettle Fairy

THE SONG OF
THE CELANDINE FAIRY

Before the hawthorn leaves unfold,
Or buttercups put forth their gold,
By every sunny footpath shine
The stars of Lesser Celandine.

The Celandine Fairy

THE SONG OF
THE WILLOW-CATKIN FAIRY

The people call me Palm, they do;
They call me Pussy-Willow too.
And when I'm full in bloom, the bees
Come humming round my yellow trees.

The people trample round about
And spoil the little trees, and shout;
My shiny twigs are thin and brown:
The people pull and break them down.
To keep a Holy Feast, they say,
They take my pretty boughs away.
I should be glad—I should not mind—
If only people weren't unkind.

Oh, you may pick a piece, you may
(So dear and silky, soft and grey);
But if you're rough and greedy, why
You'll make the little fairies cry.

(This catkin is the flower of the Sallow Willow.)

The Willow-Catkin Fairy

THE SONG OF
THE GROUNDSEL FAIRY

If dicky-birds should buy and sell
In tiny markets, I can tell
   The way they'd spend their money.
They'd ask the price of cherries sweet,
They'd choose the pinkest worms for meat,
And common Groundsel for a treat,
   Though *you* might think it funny.

Love me not, or love me well;
That's the way they'd buy and sell.

The Groundsel Fairy

THE SONG OF
THE WINDFLOWER FAIRY

While human-folk slumber,
  The fairies espy
Stars without number
  Sprinkling the sky.

The Winter's long sleeping,
  Like night-time, is done;
But day-stars are leaping
  To welcome the sun.

Star-like they sprinkle
  The wildwood with light;
Countless they twinkle—
  The Windflowers white!

(" Windflower " is another name for Wood Anemone.)

The Windflower Fairy

THE SONG OF
THE SHEPHERD'S-PURSE FAIRY

Though I'm poor to human eyes
Really I am rich and wise.
Every tiny flower I shed
Leaves a heart-shaped purse instead.

In each purse is wealth indeed—
Every coin a living seed.
Sow the seed upon the earth—
Living plants shall spring to birth.

Silly people's purses hold
Lifeless silver, clinking gold;
But you cannot grow a pound
From a farthing in the ground.

Money may become a curse:
Give me then my Shepherd's Purse.

The Shepherd's-Purse Fairy

THE SONG OF
THE DAISY FAIRY

Come to me and play with me,
   I'm the babies' flower;
Make a necklace gay with me,
Spend the whole long day with me,
   Till the sunset hour.

I must say Good-night, you know,
   Till tomorrow's playtime;
Close my petals tight, you know,
Shut the red and white, you know,
   Sleeping till the daytime.

The Daisy Fairy

THE SONG OF
THE DANDELION FAIRY

Here's the Dandelion's rhyme:
   See my leaves with tooth-like edges;
Blow my clocks to tell the time;
   See me flaunting by the hedges,
In the meadow, in the lane,
   Gay and naughty in the garden;
Pull me up—I grow again,
   Asking neither leave nor pardon.
Sillies, what are you about
   With your spades and hoes of iron?
You can never drive me out—
   Me, the dauntless Dandelion!

The Dandelion Fairy

THE SONG OF
THE DAFFODIL FAIRY

I'm everyone's darling: the blackbird and
    starling
Are shouting about me from blossoming
    boughs;
For I, the Lent Lily, the Daffy-down-dilly,
Have heard through the country the call to
    arouse.
The orchards are ringing with voices
    a-singing
The praise of my petticoat, praise of my
    gown;
The children are playing, and hark! they are
    saying
That Daffy-down-dilly is come up to town!

The Daffodil Fairy

THE SONG OF
THE DOG-VIOLET FAIRY

The wren and robin hop around;
    The Primrose-maids my neighbours be;
The sun has warmed the mossy ground;
Where Spring has come, I too am found:
    The Cuckoo's call has wakened me!

The Dog-Violet Fairy

THE SONG OF
THE PRIMROSE FAIRY

The Primrose opens wide in spring;
 Her scent is sweet and good:
It smells of every happy thing
 In sunny lane and wood.
I have not half the skill to sing
 And praise her as I should.

She's dear to folk throughout the land;
 In her is nothing mean:
She freely spreads on every hand
 Her petals pale and clean.
And though she's neither proud nor grand,
 She is the Country Queen.

The Primrose Fairy

THE SONG OF
THE LADY'S SMOCK FAIRY

Where the grass is damp and green,
Where the shallow streams are flowing,
Where the cowslip buds are showing,
  I am seen.

Dainty as a fairy's frock,
White or mauve, of elfin sewing,
'Tis the meadow-maiden growing—
  Lady's Smock.

The Lady's Smock Fairy

THE SONG OF
THE LARCH FAIRY

Sing a song of Larch trees
    Loved by fairy-folk;
Dark stands the pinewood,
    Bare stands the oak,
But the Larch is dressed and trimmed
    Fit for fairy-folk!

Sing a song of Larch trees,
    Sprays that swing aloft,
Pink tufts, and tassels
    Grass-green and soft:
All to please the little elves
    Singing songs aloft!

The Larch Fairy

THE SONG OF
THE BLUEBELL FAIRY

My hundred thousand bells of blue,
  The splendour of the Spring,
They carpet all the woods anew
With royalty of sapphire hue;
The Primrose is the Queen, 'tis true.
  But surely I am King!
    Ah, yes,
  The peerless Woodland King!

Loud, loud the thrushes sing their song;
  The bluebell woods are wide;
My stems are tall and straight and strong;
From ugly streets the children throng,
They gather armfuls, great and long,
  Then home they troop in pride—
    Ah yes,
  With laughter and with pride!

(This is the Wild Hyacinth. The Bluebell of Scotland is the
Harebell.)

The Bluebell Fairy

THE SONG OF
THE STITCHWORT FAIRY

I am brittle-stemmed and slender,
But the grass is my defender.

On the banks where grass is long,
I can stand erect and strong.

All my mass of starry faces
Looking up from wayside places,

From the thick and tangled grass,
Gives you greeting as you pass.

(A prettier name for Stitchwort is Starwort, but it is not so
often used.)

The Stitchwort Fairy

THE SONG OF
THE WOOD-SORREL FAIRY

In the wood the trees are tall,
    Up and up they tower;
You and I are very small—
    Fairy-child and flower.

Bracken stalks are shooting high,
    Far and far above us;
We are little, you and I,
    But the fairies love us.

The Wood-Sorrel Fairy

THE SONG OF
THE SPEEDWELL FAIRY

Clear blue are the skies;
  My petals are blue;
  As beautiful, too,
As bluest of eyes.

The heavens are high:
  By the field-path I grow
  Where wayfarers go,
And " Good speed," say I;

" See, here is a prize
  Of wonderful worth:
  A weed of the earth,
As blue as the skies!"

(There are many kinds of Speedwell: this is the Germander.)

The Speedwell Fairy

THE SONG OF
THE LORDS-AND-LADIES FAIRY

Here's the song of Lords-and-Ladies (in the
    damp and shade he grows):
I have neither bells nor petals, like the fox-
    glove or the rose.
Through the length and breadth of England,
    many flowers you may see—
Petals, bells, and cups in plenty—but there's
    no one else like me.

In the hot-house dwells my kinsman, Arum-
    lily, white and fine;
I am not so tall and stately, but the quaintest
    hood is mine;
And my glossy leaves are handsome; I've a
    spike to make you stare;
And my berries are a glory in September,
    (*but beware!*)

(The Wild Arum has other names besides Lords-and-Ladies,
such as Cuckoo-Pint and Jack-in-the-Pulpit.)

The Lords-and-Ladies Fairy

THE SONG OF
THE COWSLIP FAIRY

The land is full of happy birds
And flocks of sheep and grazing herds.

I hear the songs of larks that fly
Above me in the breezy sky.

I hear the little lambkins bleat;
My honey-scent is rich and sweet.

Beneath the sun I dance and play
In April and in merry May.

The grass is green as green can be;
The children shout at sight of me.

The Cowslip Fairy

THE SONG OF
THE HEART'S-EASE FAIRY

Like the richest velvet (I've heard the fairies
    tell)
  Grow the handsome pansies within the
    garden wall;
When you praise their beauty, remember me
    as well—
  Think of little Heart's-ease, the brother of
    them all!

Come away and seek me when the year is
    young,
  Through the open ploughlands beyond the
    garden wall;
Many names are pretty and many songs are
    sung:
  Mine — because   I'm   Heart's-ease — are
    prettiest of all!

(An old lady says that when she was a little girl the children's
name for the Heart's-ease or Wild Pansy was Jump-up-and-
kiss-me!)

The Hearts-Ease Fairy

THE SONG OF
THE MAY FAIRY

My buds, they cluster small and green;
   The sunshine gaineth heat:
Soon shall the hawthorn tree be clothed
   As with a snowy sheet.

O magic sight, the hedge is white,
   My scent is very sweet;
And lo, where I am come indeed,
   The Spring and Summer meet.

The May Fairy